MY LiTTLE **PONY**

Equestria Girls

CANTERLOT HiGH

Tell-All

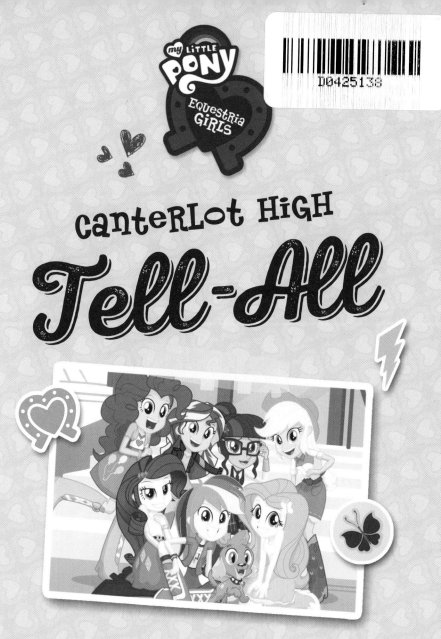

studio **fun**
A READER'S DIGEST COMPANY

White Plains, New York • Montréal, Québec • Bath, United Kingdom

Meet tHe Mane GiRLS of CanteRLot HiGH

EG

Rarity

Rarity here. I think this Tell-All book will really help Twilight Sparkle when she transfers in from Crystal Prep. I will help make sure she always puts her right foot forward—and that it will have the latest in footwear on it!

Pinkie Pie

I am always ready to have some fun and I can't wait to show Twilight Sparkle how to have a great time at Canterlot High! I plan to help her loosen up a little and laugh a lot!

Rainbow Dash

This school really rocks. And talk about team spirit! There are so many ways Twilight Sparkle can join in and become one of us. I'll introduce her to music and sports opportunities, for sure!

Sunset Shimmer

I am still learning a lot about myself but I am sure that I don't know what I'd do without my friends—so I plan to be one to Twilight Sparkle.

EQUESTRIA Girls!

Rarity No matter what challenges a day may bring, we all are fabulous together!

Rainbow Dash We are like a great sports team—stronger together than we are alone.

Being kind to each other makes great magic happen. *Fluttershy*

Applejack Honestly, we are the best of the best.

We have been through a lot but always come out laughing and happy! Pinkie Pie

What a difference strong friendships make in a girl's life! Enemies can become friends and turn the darkness into light! Sunset Shimmer

Twilight Sparkle

There's something magical about us all being together. I'm looking forward to seeing our friendship grow.

I loved the slumber party that included my little animal friends—they were so cute all curled up in little doll beds! *Fluttershy*

EG

I had a blast at the slumber party where the Rainbooms played all night long! Sunset Shimmer

Any slumber party where we are all together!

Pinkie Pie

My invitation -PP

Let's Party!

PARTY Girl!

Best Slumber Party Ever!

That one we had when I gave all of my besties a personal glam session! We never got to sleep! — Rarity

SUPER STAR

I loved being up all night playing video games with Rainbow Dash!
Applejack

I still say I won that last game!
— "Rainbox" Dash

EQUESTRIA GIRLS

How to Beat the Rainy-Day Blues

Sweet!

Rarity
I either stay in and sketch out new designs for my next fashion show, or I go outside wearing my latest stormy weather wardrobe!

EG

Sunset Shimmer
You just might find me writing to Princess Twilight Sparkle or Princess Celestia in Equestria.

Rainbow Dash
I'll be shredding my guitar and rockin' to music!

I never want to see a Venus flytrap again! As far as I'm concerned they need to stay far away and be well fed!

Rainbow Dash

I'd be very happy to never be in the spotlight on stage again when I'm not prepared!

Fluttershy

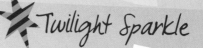

Twilight Sparkle

I don't ever want to turn into Midnight Sparkle again!

NO DAZZLINGS!

I don't ever want to deal with the Dazzlings again! No, thank you!

Applejack

CHS

I never ever, ever want to be an evil she-devil again.

Sunset Shimmer

THINGS I'D BE HAPPY TO NEVER DO AGAIN

Rarity
No need to ever fight the powers of evil magic again. My wardrobe could barely handle it.

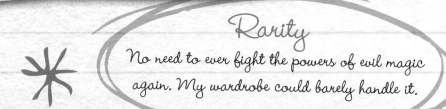

So, I don't want to ever have a beautiful party planned for Fluttershy for a Saturday again, only to find out that her birthday was Friday!

Pinkie Pie

(But the party on Saturday was such a surprise!) 💜

—Fluttershy

At the Friendship Games after I got the party started! Confetti, music, cupcakes...it wasn't just party time, it was floatie time!
Pinkie Pie

Who remembers the time when I was singing the "Wondercolts" song, getting everyone motivated for the Friendship Games? I did it without even playing my guitar!

AWESOMENESS! Rainbow Dash

FRIENDSHIP YOU shine!

Every time I "pony up," it's my favorite time!
Applejack

At the Battle of the Bands! It was the most fabulous "pony up" ever with all of us together, including Twilight from Equestria!

Rarity

Me too. It was my first time.
—Sunset Shimmer

Fluttershy I think it was when baby eagles landed on our heads!

Yeah! And one thought my hair was its nest! Since when are eagle nests pink?
—PP

Applejack When I hit that bull's-eye...and it was a spinning target!

It shocked me when Pinkie Pie burst out of the cake she made for my birthday! Sunset Shimmer

Twilight Sparkle

When everybody from CHS already knew who I was! Oh, and when Spike started talking, that was really surprising.

How about that look in Sour Sweet's eyes when I spoke to her on the archery field! Talk about big surprises!
—Spike

THE BIGGEST SURPRISE I EVER HAD WAS...

When Pinkie Pie and I were speed skating and crossed the finish line the same time as the Shadow Bolts. I'd never skated backward before, but I was so determined to win for us, that I just turned around and made that beautiful move! *Rarity*

Pinkie Pie When that party cannon went off by mistake! Still sorry about that.

When I started to "pony up" and I wasn't even singing. We were all just together and the friendship was magic! *Rainbow Dash*

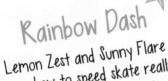

Rainbow Dash

Lemon Zest and Sunny Flare know how to speed skate really well. But when it comes to team spirit...um...not so great.

Lemon Zest sure loves her music!
—DJ Pon

More sour than sweet! That's for sure!
—PP

I thought I was a quiet talker...I'm shouting compared to her!
Fluttershy

Did someone say "robots"?
    Pinkie Pie

Love the flames.
    —DJ Pon

SUPER STAR

At first I thought they were real meanies. But they finally realized that friendship is magic!
Fluttershy

Dreadful uniforms!
Rarity

They act all hoity-toity. But they're not **all that!**
Rainbow Dash

Hey CP, how would you like some Venus flytraps for your school lawn!?
Sunset Shimmer

At first I wondered, what in tarnation was wrong with all of them, including Indigo Zap? She finally came around...they all did, pretty much.
Applejack

CRYSTAL PREP STUDENTS

The best thing about CP! —AJ

SHE ROCKS! —RD

My fave CP student!
—Rarity

Rainbow Dash
The motocross race with Sunset Shimmer!
That was **so awesome** when she
made the winning jump!

SHADOW Bolts

Applejack
The very end of
the games when
CP kids were no
longer our enemies!
And I loved doing
archery. Bull's-eye!

I **knew** I should have carried
the three in that math equation!
Sunset Shimmer

The whole thing was so strange.
And it was hard for me to play
for CP because they don't like me.
Twilight Sparkle

Friendship
EG Games

Memories of the Friendship Games

CHS hosted the Friendship Games this year. The events were an academic decathlon, a tri-cross relay, and a tie-breaking round of capture the flag.

—Rainbow Dash

Rarity All of the fantastic sports outfits I put together so we would look and feel our best when we competed against our rival school, Crystal Prep. Oh, and skating around that mean curve with Pinkie Pie!

WONDER Colts

How about that double soufflé we made, right Fluttershy?

Pinkie Pie

Still can't figure out how we did that!

—Fluttershy

Forgiveness.
No question!
Sunset Shimmer

♡ ♡ ♡ ♡ ♡ ♡

Applejack
Fancy cowboy
boots.

FOLDING YOUR COOTIE CATCHER

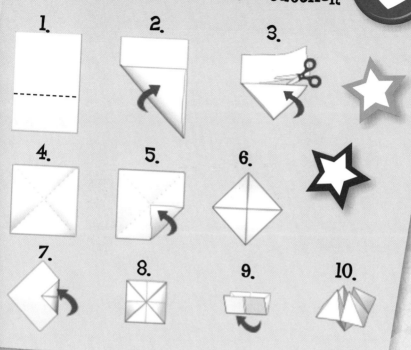

1.

2.

3.

4.

5.

6.

7.

8.

9.

10.

HOW TO MAKE YOUR COOTIE CATCHER

1. Cut the cootie catcher out as shown.
2. Fold the left corner up to meet the right side.
3. Fold the right corner up to meet the left side and cut off the top as shown.
4. Unfold the paper and place it printed side down.
5. Fold up all four corners so that they meet in the middle, as shown.
6. It should look like this. Now, flip it over.
7. Fold up all four corners, as shown.
8. Now, it should look like this.
9. Fold the catcher in half.
10. Slide your thumbs and fingers under the four flaps. You are now ready to use the cootie catcher and get a message from Twilight Sparkle in Equestria!

Rarity
My beautiful new sewing machine! It's perfect!

Fluttershy
The fence my friends put up in my backyard to make it a safe place for all my animals.

Lifetime gift card at the party store!

Pinkie Pie

Rainbow Dash
A rainbow-striped tracksuit!

Bright Star

8

1

2

you will rock
out like a Rainbow

you will make
a new friend

you are as
sweet as one of
APPLEJACK'S Pies

you will ace
your next test

The Magic
of Friendship
is everywhere

Somepony has a
crush on you

7

4

you can make
the sun shine

Someone will
throw you a
Pinkie Pie Party

6

5

3

HOW to USE YOUR Cootie Catcher

STEP 1: Find a friend. Ask her to pick one of the colored hearts on the top of the cootie catcher. Work the cootie catcher back and forth as you spell out the letters in the color (p-i-n-k).

STEP 2: Now ask your friend to pick one of the numbers on view inside the paper fortune-teller. Then work the cootie catcher back and forth again as you count up to the number (1, 2, 3, 4).

STEP 3: Ask your friend to pick one of the numbers on view inside the cootie catcher. Then raise up the flap to read Twilight's message!

WHAT TWILIGHT SPARKLE IN EQUESTRIA WANTS YOU TO KNOW...

She wants you to make this cool cootie catcher to get some special messages from her!

IF I COULD ASK TWILIGHT SPARKLE IN EQUESTRIA JUST ONE THING...

Rarity

Oh, I'd love to know what's the latest fashion trend in Equestria.

I'd like to know what music is really popular there right now.
Rainbow Dash

How can we make all the students at CP appreciate the magic of friendship?
♡ Pinkie Pie

Applejack
When can we see you again?

Sunset Shimmer
Can we write to each other more?

Twilight Sparkle

It's so strange but I feel like we've known each other for a very long time!

MY FAVORITE THING ABOUT TWILIGHT SPARKLE FROM CRYSTAL PREP

Her passion for purple gives her a bit of princess pizazz! Too bad she is stuck wearing that CP uniform for now.
Rarity

She is awesome! I know I can count on her when I need an answer to a tough question!
Rainbow Dash

That she is open to making real friends—I know how hard that can be!
Sunset Shimmer

Pinkie Pie
Last week she discovered a gazillion new ways to make animal balloons!

Fluttershy
I can't wait until she's at CHS with us.

Bright STAR

Honestly, I always like it when Twilight Sparkle is around! Our friendship circle feels more complete when she's here! **Applejack**

Rarity

Best thing, and I know I am repeating myself (but this is worth repeating), is that she saved the whole school from those evil Dazzlings!

Rainbow Dash She's really great at spelling...or is that spells?

I know she is trying really hard to make up for her past mistakes.

Pinkie Pie

Sunset Shimmer never gives up when there's a problem. She always figures out a way to solve it.

Fluttershy

Applejack

That girl owned up to what she did wrong and tries to do better every day. She can hold her head up high!

Oh gosh, I'm blushing!

—Sunset Shimmer

Fluttershy

I love going to her house and seeing all the animals in her barn. I bring them apples!

EQUESTRIA GIRLS

LOVE

We had **so much fun** painting balloons on her bedroom wall! Pinkie Pie

I love having everyone over! We make apple pies, apple breads, and apple muffins. And we drink it all down with apple cider!

Applejack

Everything in her bedroom wa already so nicely coordinated i apple red and green!

Rarity

The acoustics in her house are booming!

Rainbow Dash

> The outfit she made for me was super adorbs!
> Sunset Shimmer

It was so nice when Rarity told me that my green outfit brought out my true inner beauty. Fluttershy

Applejack I had a blast until the audience tossed roses up onto the stage and one of them accidentally landed in my eye. Ouch.

EG

Dress-Up!

Cut out along the dotted line.
Use the stickers to dress up the girls.

at Rarity's Last Fashion Show

I was overwhelmed by how great the audience's reaction was to my newest collection, which I call *Fabulous Friendship Fashion*—and that my friends modeled!

♥ Rarity

Rarity scored some major fashion points with the outfit she made for me. Except she had me wear magnetic hair clips and my head got stuck on a metal wall!

Rainbow Dash

Pinkie Pie
I misunderstood and thought I was supposed to run down the runway and then I bumped into Rainbow Dash, and she fell on Fluttershy!

EG

I'm trying to forget that!
—RD

She's breathtaking with power chords! *Rarity*

Pinkie Pie I get so *nervouscited* when I watch her compete! She's the **real deal** when it comes to sportsmanship!

She is an amazing competitor but she stopped her ride during the Friendship Games motocross race to save Sunset Shimmer from that crazy plant!
—Indigo Zap

She's the absolute best at soccer! And I'm so glad only the ball gets hit so hard! *Fluttershy*

I like to see her compete in just about any game, but especially video games. She even wins those!
Applejack

Sunset Shimmer

I'll root for Rainbow Dash no matter what she competes in. She's always been a real champion to me—even before she saved me in the motocross race!

Rainbow Dash

about Fluttershy's animal Friends

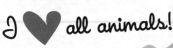

Fluttershy

Rarity

Have you ever made an outfit for a bunny? It took me a while to figure out what to do about the tail!

I ♥ all animals!

Pinkie Pie

One time I tried to get a bunch of her butterflies to fly out of a cake. Still working on that one...

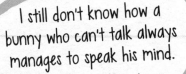

I still don't know how a bunny who can't talk always manages to speak his mind.

Rainbow Dash

Applejack

She hangs out with so many fantastic critters! Last weekend I had a nice conversation with Elizabeak. Such a friendly chicken! Oh, and I just planted some special carrots for Angel.

Last summer I babysat her bunny—and a guinea pig, a bird, two otters, a bear, seven ladybugs, an alligator, and a snake—when she went away for a weekend.

Sunset Shimmer

Fluttershy

The food is always so tasty! I also take some home to my animal friends.

Applejack

That Pinkie Pie sure knows how to throw a party. We all get up and dance, even if there's no music!

Twilight Sparkle
I am so looking forward to being invited to these!

Sunset Shimmer

I like the pics we take! Look at his selfie from the last party!

My Fav Thing about Pinkie Pie's Parties

We have a blast getting ready and I love "fabulizing" everyone. I think I speak for all of us when I say that that's as much fun as the party itself! Rarity

They're always fun! Sometimes I laugh so hard, tears stream down my face!

Rainbow Dash

Pinkie Pie

My fav thing is the balloons! The cake! The music! Oh, the confetti! No, sillies. The best part of any party is my friends!

Discover your Canterlot High Personality

Which of the girls at Canterlot High are you the most like? Take this quiz and find out!

1. My favorite thing about a party is:
   A. when I surprise everyone with my singing
   B. dancing
   C. everything
   D. playing games
   E. meeting nice people
   F. dressing up

2. I would love to have the biggest collection of:
   A. guitars
   B. boots
   C. party decorations
   D. trophies
   E. stuffed animals
   F. jewelry

3. When I go to bed I think about:
   A. whether I was a good friend
   B. riding a horse
   C. cake
   D. playing soccer
   E. planting a garden
   F. what I'm going to wear tomorrow

4. My feelings get hurt sometimes when people:
   A. don't accept my apology
   B. tell me I talk with an accent
   C. turn down an invitation
   D. are sore losers
   E. ignore my pets
   F. don't appreciate my advice

5. It's fun to remember the best times I had:
   A. singing with friends
   B. picking apples
   C. baking
   D. shredding guitar
   E. going to the park
   F. shopping

6. If I had to pick one symbol to describe me, it would be:
   A. the sun
   B. a red apple
   C. a balloon
   D. the rainbow
   E. a butterfly
   F. a diamond

7. My favorite color is:
  A. orange
  B. red
  C. pink
  D. all the colors of the rainbow
  E. green
  F. purple

8. My dream vacation:
  A. sunny, tropical paradise
  B. any place with horses and hayrides
  C. Mardi Gras
  D. ski resort
  E. rainforest ecotour
  F. Paris or New York

9. I would bring this on a picnic:
  A. grill and charcoal
  B. apple spice muffins
  C. cupcakes
  D. softball and bat
  E. camera
  F. fancy tablecloth and napkins

10. Favorite subject in school:
  A. music
  B. history
  C. home economics
  D. gym
  E. earth science
  F. arts and crafts

ANSWER KEY

If you picked mostly:
A: You are like Sunset Shimmer
B: You are like Applejack
C: You are like Pinkie Pie
D: You are like Rainbow Dash
E: You are like Fluttershy
F: You are like Rarity

Fluttershy

I hope to be a veterinarian. And I also want to run my own animal shelter for ladybugs and other animals.

Sunset Shimmer

Instead of taking over the world, I'd like to travel and see it! And also develop apps!

Applejack

I plan to get a degree in environmental science and put it to good use back home!

Twilight Sparkle

I either want to be a scientist or an engineer.

ifT HERE
OR QUIZ!

WHAT I'D LIKE TO DO after COLLEGE

Rarity

Open lots of clothing stores featuring designs by me, and create fabulous fashions for movie stars!

Rainbow Dash

Maybe I'll coach soccer. Or motocross. Or archery. Or, maybe I'll form **an awesome band**!

Pinkie Pie

I'm going to be a party planner. Of course! Ooooh, wait. Maybe I'll be a professional drummer. Or a drumming party planner!

Rainbow Dash I wish I could score the winning point in a tied championship match—the sport doesn't matter!

How AWESOME would that be?!

SUPER STAR

Fluttershy Oh, how I wish I had time to have a conversation with every animal I see!

I wish I could have a big helping of my grandma's apple pie for breakfast, lunch, and dinner! **Applejack**

EG

I wish that there would be no more evil magic ever again. Just good magic.

Sunset Shimmer

I WiSH...

Rarity I dream of being a famous fashion designer someday, hobnobbing with the top designers in the business.

That everyone would make time to relax and have a party every now and then!

Pinkie Pie

Fluttershy

I'm terrified of being in the spotlight in front of a crowd. Except when we sing together.

Applejack

Sometimes I start thinking about my besties and I get afraid that we might drift apart one day. But I honestly don't think that will happen.

Sunset Shimmer

I'm terrified that I'll never be forgiven for being so rotten.

Right on!
Friends forever!
—Sunset Shimmer

We forgive you!
We forgive you!
—PP

Twilight Sparkle

I am afraid that Spike will get lost!!

I'm with you always!
—Spike

BFF

Rarity
That I'll miss out on a single second of being with my best friends.

Pinkie Pie That all the balloons in the world will pop at the same time!

I'm not afraid of much. Well, okay, I am afraid of being cooped up inside for too long...oh, and of falling asleep in class!
Rainbow Dash

Sweet!

Rarity Okay, I'm not going to say who my crush is... but I know a certain little purple someone who is back in Equestria and who has a crush on me!

Rainbow Dash That guy on the baseball team. I don't even know his name. But when he caught that fly ball the other day, WOW!

Pinkie Pie I'm going to write this really fast because it's a confession...Shining Armor. There I said it. Sh-h-h-h.

Fluttershy Oh, boy! That earthy guy who plays in the Green Cycle band. I'm too shy to let him know that he gives me butterflies!

Applejack I do have a crush. My childhood friend Jonathan, who grew up on the apple farm right next door to mine!

Sunset Shimmer I don't really have a crush right now. Since Flash and I broke up, I haven't really liked anyone. But I'm hoping that will change soon!

XOXO

Pinkie Pie
They fed off negativity.
Can't get much worse than that!

Fluttershy
They acted nice to our faces, but were big phonies.

EVERYTHING!
Except that I got a chance to prove I'm a loyal friend.

Sunset Shimmer

They used their magic in a really bad way and got the whole school under their spell. It was hard at first, but together we were able to overcome them and their evil ways!

Applejack

THE WORST THING ABOUT THE DAZZLINGS

They were so bad that StarSwirl the Bearded banished them from Equestria long ago. They were just simply **dreadful!** *Rarity*

Rainbow Dash

They were awful musicians! Did you hear them try to sing without their musical pendants?

Give me a break!

Fluttershy

It has to be "Rainbow Rocks"! Each time we sing it, I like it **more.**

EG

Applejack

I love "Shake Your Tail." It makes me so happy! And I shake my tail when I sing it! We're here to have a party tonight!

RAINBOOMS

Sunset Shimmer

"My Past Is Not Today"

♡ ♡ ♡ ♡ ♡ ♡

My Favorite Song

Right now it's "Life Is a Runway!" But I loved every song we sang when we had Twilight Sparkle from Equestria on stage with us!

Rarity

♡ ♥ Pinkie Pie

Lately I've been singing "Perfect Day for Fun...La la la...With my best friends, we can depend!"

Rainbow Dash

Any song where I get to shred my guitar is my fave!

Rarity Of course we looked and sounded fantastic, but none of that would have mattered without Sunset Shimmer. Without her, we would not have been able to defeat that evil band, the Dazzlings—she saved everyone from falling under their spell.

I loved being on stage. And when we ponied up...that was totally awesome! Twilight from Equestria was the first to realize that it was the Magic of Friendship and us being in harmony as friends that makes us pony up!
Rainbow Dash

Pinkie Pie I remember when we had a face-off with Trixie and we won!

After Snips and Snails scared me with the spotlight, I found a way to work up my courage for the real performance that night. **Fluttershy**

Applejack The cheers from the audience! We rocked it! And when Sunset Shimmer sang, we were totally complete as a group!

It felt great singing with the Rainbooms! That's when the real magic happened!
Sunset Shimmer

REMEMBERING tHE BATTLE of tHE BANDS

LOVE THIS!

Sweet!

We formed the Rainbooms with Twilight Sparkle from Equestria initially to compete in the Battle of the Bands, but kept playing together with Sunset Shimmer because we totally ROCK!

Rainbow Dash

The Rainbooms really rock!
Applejack

FOR tHE FRiENDSHiP GaMES SHOWCaSE, WE HaD:

Rainbow Dash on guitar and vocals
Rarity on keytar
Fluttershy on tambourine
Applejack on bass
Pinkie Pie on drums
Sunset Shimmer on guitar

Cut here

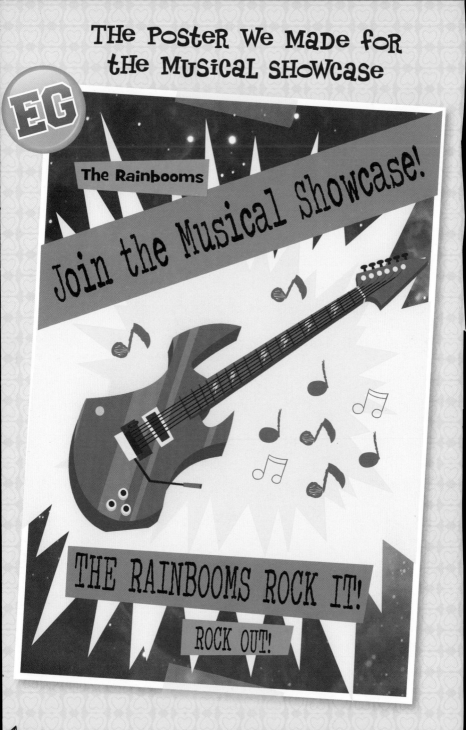

OPEN HERE tO DESIGN YOUR OWN POSTER USING tHE STICKERS!

THE RAINBOOMS

SUPER STAR

We are all rehearsed and ready!
Pinkie Pie

Pinkie Pie

The city, for sure! So many parties and restaurants! And the lights were a never-ending celebration! I could have stayed there a whole month! Or a year!

Fluttershy

I still think about our trip to the zoo. I loved every single second of it.

Applejack

How fun was that hayride at the farm when we were all together?! Had a blast, even though I forgot to take the apple pie home!

Sunset Shimmer

Can't wait to go back to the park. The hike, the picnic, and the rainstorm...all memorable!

The pie was delish!
-PP

My Favorite Class Trip

Rarity

The Adventure Park, even though I'm still getting over when the Ferris wheel got stuck at the top! It was so windy that my hair kept getting messed up!

One of my favorite days with my besties! —Rarity

Rainbow Dash

That Sports Museum was off the charts! I was especially blown away walking down the Hall of Fame. I hope my picture will be up there one day!

We had so much fun dancing together! And I framed my copy of the group photo we took with Twilight Sparkle from Equestria after she was named Princess of the Formal. *Fluttershy*

I had as much fun planning it as I did going to it! I picked out the decorations and had SOOO much fun making the cake!

Pinkie Pie

Loved the dancing, too, Fluttershy. But is no one going to mention what went on with Sunset Shimmer?!

Applejack

You mentioned it, Applejack! I'd rather forget how I turned into a raving "she-demon!" Literally. I'm never going to live that down. Sunset Shimmer

Memories from the Fall Formal

Remember when I almost... almost didn't finish everyone's outfits in time?! I did it, though, and we all looked like princesses!

Rarity

This year was our best fall formal ever I loved how we helped each other get ready! Still sorry I spilled my cup of red punch on you, Pinkie Pie!

Rainbow Dash

Oh, that's okay, Rainbow Dash. It matched my dress! —PP

Rarity Oh dear, how will I choose between the animal print or the tropical print shirt? The formfitting or flowing skirt?

Rainbow Dash Anything SPORTY!

Pinkie Pie My blue heart!

Fluttershy I have a green butterfly for our class pics. And my butterfly clip!

Applejack I love to wear my denim skirt and green shirt. Okay, I love to wear that every day!

Twilight Sparkle Anything purple!

Yee-haw!

Sunset Shimmer My favorite jacket.

My Favorite Outfit for the School Picture

CANTERLOT HIGH

Rarity

Pinkie Pie

Fluttershy

Applejack

Fluttershy

Bird Seed. I bring some every day to feed the birds outside in the school yard.

Sunset Shimmer

My water bottle. I always grab it before leaving the house!

Applejack

A bandanna. Gotta have it.

You've got to have a banana? —PP

Bandanna, silly! **Ban-dan-na!** —AJ

SPIKE! ♡

I can't go to SCHOOL WithOut...

Rarity

Oh that's easy. My charm bracelet. Oh, and my little mirror—the one with my initials on it. And nail polish for touch-ups. And a needle and thread. Just in case.

Pinkie Pie

No one knows this, but I always make sure I have a bag of confetti in my locker. Just in case...

Rainbow Dash

My running shoes! Oh, and an energy bar, especially if I'm staying late for a game.

Sweetie Belle

I love dressing up for school. And I especially love art class. But yesterday I got in trouble for talking too much while we were painting.

It can be kind of embarrassing to have your little sister in the same hallway at school! But, honestly darling, I couldn't have asked for a better little sister—you are a real gem! —Rarity

I think it's awesome that I can hop on my scooter and ride it to CHS every day. Okay, I probably should NOT have ridden it in the halls. I almost rode right into Twilight Sparkle from Equestria! But she was really nice about it. Most of the older kids are nice to us. Especially when Apple Bloom, Sweetie Belle, and I play our music together! Scootaloo

THE FRESHMAN CLASS WEIGHS IN

Scootaloo

Sweetie Belle!

I'm just getting used to being in CHS with the older kids. It's more and more fun every day. My friend Sweetie Belle sits next to me in science class and we both have a total crush on the boy in front of us.

(Shhhh, don't tell him, you guys!)

Apple Bloom

Rarity

Fashion Club! So far, this year I've made 27 costumes for our runway shows. I know I'm behind where I was last year, so I better get sewing!

Rainbow Dash

Music Club. When the Rainbooms band isn't practicing or playing, Music Club rocks!

Fluttershy

I love the Outdoor Club. Last weekend we planted trees. Next week we're going on a hike with a butterfly expert!

Thanks for all those trees!
—Spike

Pinkie Pie

I was voted president of the Baking Club—again! I've just decided that every Friday is "Sweet Treat Day!" It's a day to bring in home-baked goods and share them!

Sunset Shimmer

I just joined the Movie Club. I really like those high-action films—better to see those things on the screen than in real life, I've decided!

Applejack

Dance Club! Dance Club! Practicing my country two-step for the hoedown at the country fair!

MY FAVORITE SCHOOL CLUB

Go Team

Twilight Sparkle
When I transfer to CHS, I am going to make sure to sign up for the Science and Technology Club.

C'mon CHS...
shake your tails
—RD

Fluttershy

I sit outside under a tree and listen to the birds. Usually, my adorable Angel is on my lap and we study together.

Anywhere it is really quiet and I can concentrate—so it's usually at home, after school.

Sunset Shimmer

☆ ☆ ☆

Applejack

I listen to my favorite country tunes. I have the best earbuds that block out other noise—it's the only way.

Twilight Sparkle

Some students meet for study group, but I prefer to be alone with Spike. He's like my studying assistant.

HOW I STUDY FOR A TEST

Pinkie Pie

Focus, focus, focus. No thoughts of parties, cupcakes, balloons, or my friends.

Uhm, what was the question?

Rarity

Studying is the only time I seek comfort over style.

When I study for a test, I play my guitar between every chapter that I have to review. The harder the test is going to be, the more I shred!

Rainbow Dash

A+ excellent

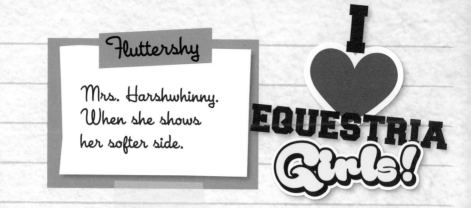

Fluttershy

Mrs. Harshwhinny.
When she shows
her softer side.

Sunset Shimmer

I like all my science teachers, but
I really wish I could find a magic
teacher in this world!

♡ ♡ ♡ ♡ ♡ ♡ ♡

SCIENCE
TEACHERS

Applejack

Well, she's not really a
teacher, but she does teach
me about life and stuff. My
grandmother, Granny Smith,
of course! Sweet to the core!

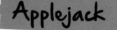

Granny Smith

MY FAVORITE TEACHER

Rarity

Definitely Miss Cheerilee. I'm pretty surprised how patient she is with us when we're in the library. Although I do think she could use a little help with her fashion sense. That green dress has got to go!

Miss Cheerilee

Pinkie Pie

Mr. Cranky Doodle. It's my mission in life to turn his frown into a smile. Maybe then his wig won't fall off in class every day!

Mr. Cranky Doodle

Rainbow Dash

Miss Clippity Clop. She's a pretty good English teacher, but I really like her because one time she started dancing in class. I love a teacher who isn't afraid to move it!

I ♥ EG

SUPER STAR

♥ ♥ ♥ ♥ ♥ ♥ ♥

I really adore geometry! It helps me enormously with pattern making.
Rarity

Pinkie Pie I have such a hard time picking a favorite, but it's probably chemistry! I love how you combine things to make something new—it reminds me of baking!

Rainbow Dash Gym class. Come on, let's go kick a soccer ball!

Fluttershy I like music class because I get to sing in the chorus. And sometimes we set my poems to music and the whole chorus sings them! And my animal friends chime in.

LOVE **Sunset Shimmer** I like math class a whole lot. Numbers never lie, so they are teaching me a lot!

Applejack I love to sink my teeth into a crunchy apple and also into history! I love finding out about the past and watching how the seeds planted long ago can impact our lives today.

She is a wonderful principal! I would just like to see her wear her hair up sometimes, though.

Rarity

Pinkie Pie

She's so sweet and nice. One afternoon she even helped me get balloons out of a tree in the schoolyard!

I like her a lot. She was so supportive during the Friendship Games, and she let me give my pep talk during the assembly.

Rainbow Dash

Not only does she do a great job here, but on the weekends she volunteers at an animal shelter.

Fluttershy

Let me just say I could not do her job. Imagine dealing with all of us every day! Especially ME. Well, the old me.

Sunset Shimmer

I like her! Just don't do anything to get her mad...then it's not pretty.

Applejack

I like her better than our principal at CP, Principal Cinch. I'm so glad she's letting me transfer to CHS.

Twilight Sparkle

Shhhhh!

Sweet!

LOVE

I love CHS, but I'd rather be on the stage, or out on the soccer field, rather than inside the classroom. I'm just sayin'...!

Rainbow Dash

Fluttershy This is the best place—it's where my friends accept me for who I am.

I'm getting to like CHS more and more every day. Today I like it a lot!

Sunset Shimmer

Applejack Besides my friends, I would have to say my favorite part of CHS is the Wondercolt statue, and the fun times we have there together, just kickin' around and laughing.

Wondercolt statue!

Twilight Sparkle
Making friends wasn't important to me at Crystal Prep. I can't wait to go from having no friends to having best friends at CHS!

Rainbow Dash

Pinkie Pie

Rarity

BFF

Rarity There's no better place to get a quality education—and a lot of it is what we teach each other!

I really, really, really love CHS. Really!!! Hey, everybody! Let's have a party to celebrate all the fun and friendships at CHS! I'll bring the cake! Did I mention that I really LOVE my school? Pinkie Pie

Fluttershy

I'm kind of shy and quiet a lot of the time and can't imagine being new somewhere! I'll make sure Twilight Sparkle has a lunch buddy.

Applejack

I'm just a country girl who likes to tell it like it is. So I'll be by Twilight Sparkle's side giving her some straight talk to help her figure things out about us and our school. But we're a pretty easy group to get to know!

Twilight Sparkle

I'm so excited to become a Wondercolt! Making friends is going to be my greatest experiment yet! I just hope I can live up to Twilight Sparkle from Equestria's reputation.

WONDER
Colts

Canterlot
High School

Twilight Sparkle